TIME IS THE MERCY OF ETERNITY

A meditation in four acts

by

Deb Margolin

SAMUEL FRENCH

FOUNDED 1830

New York Hollywood London Toronto

SAMUELFRENCH.COM

IMPORTANT BILLING AND CREDIT
REQUIREMENTS

All producers of TIME IS THE MERCY OF ETERNITY *must* give credit to the Author of the Play in all programs distributed in connection with performances of the Play, and in all instances in which the title of the Play appears for the purposes of advertising, publicizing or otherwise exploiting the Play and /or a production. The name of the Author *must* appear on a separate line on which no other name appears, immediately following the title and *must* appear in size of type not less than fifty percent of the size of the title type.

Clarisse & Larmon, act two of ***Time is the Mercy of Eternity*** was first produced at the Ignite Fesitval at the Ohio Theatre, October 4 - 22, 2007, by Synapse Productions. The play was under the direction of David Travis with the following cast:

SOLDIER	Jon Credeld
CLARISSE	Kathleen Chalfant
LARMON	Shawn Elliot

CHARACTERS

This is a quartet of pieces for a quartet of actors. The play is performed by a young woman, a young man (both mid-20s), an older woman, and an older man (both mid-50s).

The multiple casting is designed as a kind of human poetry, casting light on the imbricated conceits and thematic unity of the multiple pieces.

When They Quiet Down, I Start
Man, mid-50s as SUICIDE BOMBER

Clarisse and Larmon
Woman, mid-50s as CLARISSE
Man, mid-50s as LARMON
Man, mid-20s as THE SOLDIER

The Rich Silk of It
Woman, mid-20s as SHE
Man, mid-20s as HE/BARTENDER/PASTOR

Time Is the Mercy of Eternity
Woman, mid-50s as WOMAN IN BED
Woman, mid-20s as WOMAN IN BLAZER
Man, mid-20s as SECURITY GUARD

Act I

WHEN THEY QUIET DOWN, I START

*(Lights up on a working class man who stands, hands jammed
in his pockets, responding, perhaps, to the questions of an
unseen interviewer. He is unremarkable in appearance;
rumpled and unselfconscious in dress; you wouldn't notice
him in a crowd. He is ageless, and has the look of someone
who just got off work. He addresses the audience as if it
were one person, with an odd combination of reticence and
gusto.)*

Sure. Interesting, sure. Sure it is, it's interesting, sure. Sure it is,
it's interesting, sure. You caught me! Sure! It's a scoop! Sure!
Who the hell's gonna believe you? But sure! It's interesting, sure,
it bores the fucking gizzards outta me, but sure! It's interesting!
So, what? What you want to talk about, about this? This ain't
no Greek thing, big myth, no big religious story. I just drive
the bus! I just drive the big bus! What else you wanna know, if
it's interesting? Sure! It's very interesting! To *you!* To *you* it's
interesting! What you wanna know? I drive this bus. And I can
take groups, singles, whatever I gotta take. But that ain't what
you're interested in, it ain't! I can see that! You wanna know
about my two destinations, H&H, I call 'em, you wanna know

about the vacation spots without payin' for the vacation! I know your type, you're cheap! But I ain't talking about that, but I'll tell you about the people, you like to know about people? You like that? I'll tell you about the people. I think people are all the same, I'll tell you, I really do. How many people do ya got to read about, hear about? Every person has the same things as every other person! When people talk it just bores you, because it's just the same as everything else you ever thought about in your own mind! Think about it! When was the last time anyone ever told you something you really didn't know? Unless it was a fact about a new K-Mart or something? Eh? Really! I swear! Think about it! I'm givin' you some new information here!

I take them so called suicide bombers, that's what they call those people, suicide bombers. You wanted to know about that, didn't you? What does that mean? It means they blow up themselves in front of other people, and they blow those people up too, like going to the theater and the next thing you know you're in the show! And they're mostly men, a few girls, but mostly men. They show up here all righteous but they also cry. They carry their bodies in little baskets, little picnic baskets like. So they walk in with one body, but they carry another one. Hard to explain. The death body walks in, the life body's in the picnic basket. And they're really new at being dead, like they're real surprised at it. But that just makes as much sense as anything else, right, I mean, you're always new at being what you are right in that moment, anyway, right, what's the difference? Think about it! Every minute you stand in, like, you never stood in that moment before, right, so people are always shocked, right? It's really new all the time, is that a headache, or what? Nothing new about that! Think about it!

They cry the minute I get 'em, like little babies that can't use their eyes yet, they just cry, not for anything in particular, and they turn their heads like babies do, and they open their mouths, it's really pathetic, they cry. I just herd 'em into the bus. They have all this stuff in their pockets, and it falls out when they get in, and they never see it again. I don't see it neither after that. Usually it's just letters and coins, Bibles and a picture, maybe, of somebody, some lady, like their mother or somebody. Or a phone number. Every time there's death, this is what falls down, or out the fucking window, or they pull it out of the water. Have you noticed that? Then there's this howling, like at a gambling table when someone loses all their shit, and then they shut up finally, and then I start the bus. Then I start the bus. When they quiet down, I start. And then they remember, and they start to think about the virgins.

See, they come up here, they blow up, and they tell them they're going to get 72 virgins, that's part of what they blow up for. Can you imagine some shit like that? Now between you and me I never liked virgins much. I don't need no screamy little women going all googly and saying O that hurts or something! And then looking at you all weird afterwards with their eyes like bulletholes when you just want to watch TV, okay? It's sloppy and boring and I don't know what to say, alright? And it's such a big deal it's boring, I'd rather have someone who knew the fuck their way around the block, you follow? In other words, I'm the virgin with a virgin, not them, and it ain't fair to anybody PLUS it's boring, right? But these people came up here for the virgins, and most of them are virgins themselves, and they only have these smoky and small little ideas about what that's gonna be like, I mean, even if you like virgins, 72 is a headache, am I making sense here? And as long as I got your attention, lemme tell you something. They give the same 72 virgins to every asshole that gets up here. The same ones! And it's always people who killed people but didn't admit it! You know, Nixon is one of those virgins! Can you believe it? He's the best one we have! He wears a delicate white nightie! Looks very fetching, he does! And he bows his head, lowers his eyes, like he was praying! And he fucking volunteered! Nobody forced him! He loved that play-the-virgin shit! You know, when he was quitting and he goes: my mother was a saint! *That* shit! And they got Kissinger playing one too! He ain't crossed over yet, but he gave us his soul anyway in exchange for two countries or towns or some shit. And you people wonder why he looks like a dead dog half the time down there! I'm hoping they get Reagan a thing here once they clean him the fuck up! The same virgins for every man! It's funny!

See, I was a suicide bomber myself, alright, that's how I know so much, there's a piece of news for ya! That's how I know all that stuff, I did it myself. It's interesting, sure, it's interesting, it's a scoop, right? See, they pique your interest, they show you some movies of people! You know, people who decided to do it! They saw me every day standing around this mini mart. I used to smoke over there. So they pull me into this apartment, and they show me some movies. And the people in the movies, they're standing there, real dignified-like, and they're dressed real good, and they seem like a President or something, they stand like that, you know, and they seem dead already, like Presidents, you know. Real relaxed-like. Because you see, death! Death is really kind of a vacation spot if you think about it, like the Bahamas! So these movies, they got these guys in 'em, and they say goodbye, and they've got the Bible, and like, they're real calm and they're dressed pretty good, right? And after the movies, they give a little something to eat, and then they tell you about these 72 virgins, and all that, and I pretend I'm interested, right? Otherwise they'll think I'm queer or something, right? And they'll kill me, right? Then they tell me I'll be a martyr and everyone'll have my picture in their apartment and that's good. That's real good, now THAT's interesting! I like pictures! I like how everything just stops in a picture, I like the stopping, right, I like the way there's nothing before or after it, right, so if you only felt good for that one second, that's as long as you had to hold it, right? The thing in the picture, there's nothing before it or after it, and all you have is that! And everybody looking at it in all these apartments, right?

So I'm like, okay, okay, man, right? So I'm like, okay, so the next day they show me this weird thing I'm supposed to wear, and how it works, and what to do if I'm stopped by the soldiers, the police, whatever asshole, and we talk about where to do this, and they get out a map and show me this train station, it's used by a lot of business-like people and family-like ladies with kids going to Grandma's and shit, a busy-like place but not suspicious, and they say, real serious:

Can you do this?

And I'm like, yeah! Yeah, this is interesting, yeah, I can! Sure! I can do this.

So we make a plan, it's going to be three days later, and they tell me "come back tomorrow and make a movie." But I don't want to make a movie, I tell them, just take my picture. But they set up the camera and give me the Koran. And I put on this nice suit they gave me, and I just stood there and smiled, like at my school graduation when I was 11.

And let me say I ain't never read the Koran! I don't like the Koran! I don't like the Jesus Koran neither, they tried to get me to read that, these people rang the doorbell! And the other one, with the trees on fire neither! I don't like these sayings they got in there! And there's always mountains, I hate mountains! Everybody's up on a mountain, I hate that! I like the newspaper! I prefer the newspaper! And I like the funnies! I like the drawings! And the people act like real people in the funnies! Stupid, but for a reason! Somebody's got a reason for the stupidness of people! I like that! So they want me to make this movie, but I don't want to make no movie! Pictures ain't supposed to move, that's the perfectness of pictures! They're still, nothing stays still no more, that's the perfectness of pictures. See the movies, they act like life, but that ain't life! You see what I'm getting' at here? That ain't life! Life don't really move, anyway. It's a bunch of pictures staying still. In fact I had one of those books when I was little, and you flip the pages real fast with your thumb and they look like it's moving. Now that's real life. You see what I'm getting' at here. Can't nothing stay still so you can fucking see it? Gimme a picture anytime, don't gimme no movies. One at a time please! One at a time!

So after the movie I just lay low for a coupla days, right, and then they come for me, 5 in the morning. I had been up all night, feeling really great. Usually I sleep, I'm one of those guys that really can sleep, anywhere and anytime, right, but I stayed awake. I felt just great! I didn't watch TV or nothin. The wind was good, it was a big strong wind, but not obnoxious wind, very gentle, you know, and we have a kind of thistle-weed grows outside here, I ain't never heard the name of it, I asked some people but no one knew. But when the wind blows through this thing it whistles, like, it whistles in a way like when a man admires a woman from a distance; he whistles, but she can't hear. And it was whistling all night like that, and I felt like that too. I didn't drink nothin, either. The night passed in a really interesting way like that. Then they came for me in a little beat-up car. And I got in, they had that blow-up device for me in a little waist bag and I put it on in the car, and I had my fake passport and I had some water in a little thing. They drove me for 4 hours, til I was just about a mile from the place, and dropped me off, we didn't talk the whole time, me 'n this guy, nothing. I just got out. He nodded his head and I just got out. I had my map but I didn't need it, I just started walking, and then everything speeded up, my heart, you know, just speeded up and my walking speeded up and everything went really fast like with a tape when you don't want to see the commercials, you know. Then I don't know how, I'm at this little train station, and things are even faster, and I hear voices, *are you listening to me?* I hear voices, children's voices, and I hear this woman laughing, and I see her, she's like the one they have in the billboard for Coca Cola, real young and pretty, you know, then I hear lots of women laughing, and I'm thinking those damn virgins, it's those virgins, have I done this already? and then the train starts coming in, and it's all going so fast again and again like in the movies I can hear this *click clack* like a child's toy *click clack* and all the people run down the tracks cause it's stopping down the tracks and I knew I was supposed to pull the string I knew but I didn't I just didn't and they all ran down the tracks to get the train and then when they was all safe away far away down the track I pulled the little string. That's when everything stopped. Like taking a picture of myself. The last mind picture I have stayed really long of that Coca Cola girl, and she's so still, and I like her when she's so still, she's not a virgin, and she's very very still, and that's what I see, and now I'm here driving the bus. Listen, do you understand me here? I didn't do it for the virgins, and I didn't do it for the Gods they give you in those books, I don't even like those Gods. I did it because it makes everything STOP. In one instant. It makes everything stop!

Act II

CLARISSE AND LARMON

(Lights up on LARMON and CLARISSE, a tattered, middle-aged couple sitting at a nondescript wooden table. A SOLDIER is standing at attention before them. A photograph, unseen by the audience, is on the table at which CLARISSE and LARMON are seated. The room is like a small interrogation room: undecorated, spare, small and green in cast.)

CLARISSE. This is all you have?

SOLDIER. Yes. Yes, I'm afraid so.

LARMON. There was no other…evidence? No other…

SOLDIER. No, I'm afraid not.

LARMON. Why couldn't you have brought…brought… given us…the actual…part…instead of this…this photograph?

SOLDIER. I'm afraid it would have been…

CLARISSE. Why are you so afraid of everything?

SOLDIER. Pardon me, ma'am?

CLARISSE. You're afraid this and you're afraid that and you're afraid the other thing!

SOLDIER. Ma'am…

LARMON. Clarisse, it's just a figure of speech.

SOLDIER. I understand, Sir; she's upset…

LARMON. That's no excuse!

CLARISSE. I'm not upset!

LARMON. All we have is this knee, shin, ankle and foot, and not even the real knee, shin, ankle or foot, just a picture of them, and that's all we have left, and you're NOT UPSET?

CLARISSE. No.

LARMON. We are bereft and aggrieved and we've lost everything and all we have is this bargain basement snapshot of the lower part of one of his legs…

CLARISSE. Left leg, in case you hadn't noticed…

LARMON.…and you are not upset? You are not disturbed?

CLARISSE. You are yelling at me as if I've said something. I have not said anything.

LARMON. Well, say something!

CLARISSE. You make it sound so easy to say things!

SOLDIER. I am terribly sorry for your loss, sir. Madam. I will leave you alone now. Here is a photograph of me, and on the other side is a telephone number. Please don't hesitate to call me with any questions you may have.

(CLARISSE takes photo of soldier and drops it on the floor. CLARISSE and LARMON stare at him. He salutes and exits, SL. C & L stare at photograph of leg before them in silence)

CLARISSE. Why do you suppose…

LARMON. I can't…

CLARISSE. I don't…

(Silence, they laugh for a long time.)

LARMON. Look…

CLARISSE. Look at what?

LARMON. Look at the decline of his toes, the way they go down so evenly in height, like climbing down a mountain, or a hill, or a flight of stairs.

CLARISSE. I think they look like a xylophone, like the different notes of the xylophone.

(Silence)

LARMON. When you consider the whole thing, it looks like Italy.

CLARISSE. You only say that because they always told us in school that Italy is shaped like a boot.

LARMON. They told us that because it's true.

CLARISSE. It may be true, but that may or may not be why they told us that.

LARMON. What, dear?

CLARISSE. People have many different reasons for telling you things. Their being true is often not the reason.

LARMON. Of course. The truth is just an option.

CLARISSE. Look at his knee.

LARMON. What about it?

CLARISSE. He knelt on that knee. Knelt comes from the word knee.

LARMON. Yes! I never thought of that!

CLARISSE. I like it when parts of the body get turned into verbs!

LARMON. But in the past tense, it's always easier, because the body part is further away!

CLARISSE. Do you think so?

LARMON. *(Excited.)* Tell me some more body parts like that!

CLARISSE. Armed comes from the word arm and palmed from the word palm and muscled from the word muscle and headed from the word head and minded from the word mind.

LARMON. Yes! And did you hear about the woman who backed into an airplane propeller?

CLARISSE. No.

LARMON. *Disaster!* Haha!

(Pause)

CLARISSE. He knelt…

LARMON. From the word knee…

CLARISSE.…and made me pray for that lobster you killed.

LARMON. Bessie Behemoth.

CLARISSE. Why did you name that lobster? Why did you name it?

LARMON. I was just having fun.

CLARISSE. It upset the boy.

LARMON. I know. I'm sorry.

CLARISSE. He knelt and prayed for the soul of that lobster.

LARMON. Of Bessie. Yes.

CLARISSE. And then he apologized to things for throwing them in the garbage can.

LARMON. Did he?

CLARISSE. Yes. And he'd tell them what a beautiful thing it would be to go in the garbage! How it was the beginning of a long journey, on trucks, to open landfills, through fire and into eternity.

LARMON. He described all of that?

CLARISSE. Yes.

LARMON. Well maybe he was prescient.

CLARISSE. It sounds like a description of being condemned to Hell.

(Silence)

CLARISSE. This knee. This shin, this foot. They were inside my body once.

LARMON. Clarisse dearest…

CLARISSE. They always say putting things back in the earth is a return to where things came from, but he came from Me. From my body. He didn't come from some briar patch, or golf course, he came from ME. They should put him back.

LARMON. Dearest Clarisse…he wouldn't fit anymore…

CLARISSE. He wouldn't fit…

LARMON. I…I was thinking…when that…when that… man…was here, that…man…I was thinking: shouldn't they have covered it up…shouldn't it have been covered up, at least, with a blanket or a sheet or…or…something…wouldn't it have been more dignified…

CLARISSE. Yes! Yes it would have!

LARMON. But then I was thinking…the human body is so indecipherable when it's under something.

CLARISSE. That's why they cover it

LARMON. You mean so it looks like nothing!

CLARISSE. That's right! It looks like nothing!

LARMON. So then we would have seen nothing.

CLARISSE. Yes.

LARMON. That would have been torture. I yearn to see him.

CLARISSE. I know you do.

LARMON. But he's gone.

CLARISSE. And we have nothing.

LARMON. Nothing but this leg.

CLARISSE. This picture of a leg.

LARMON. His leg.

CLARISSE. Is it his?

LARMON. Let's look.

(They stare at the photo.)

LARMON. What do you see?

CLARISSE. Well, nothing really, just the kneecap, the shin with a bit of calf peeking around, the foot.

LARMON. The metatarsal arch.

CLARISSE. Which is that?

LARMON. *(Indicating)* This here, this swell and the corresponding part under the foot.

CLARISSE. Did his look like that? His foot?

LARMON. I don't know why, but I can't remember. I'm trying to remember his feet.

CLARISSE. It might be easier if we had a picture of both feet. Two feet when put together remind of you of the person.

LARMON. Perhaps we should call that man; maybe he has another photograph of the other foot.

CLARISSE. If he'd had a photograph of the other foot, wouldn't he have left it?

LARMON. Not necessarily.

CLARISSE. Why? Why would he not have left whatever

he had?

LARMON. Maybe he wanted to make it as easy as possible for us.

CLARISSE. It isn't easy to leave us with so little.

LARMON. He may not have known. He may have thought the less the better.

CLARISSE. How could anyone be so stupid.

LARMON. Dear, you are just upset.

CLARISSE. I am not upset.

LARMON. *(Returning to photograph.)* And look at all that hair! Look at it all! He was very manly! He had very hairy legs!

CLARISSE. When he was a baby I used to soap his shins and he would kick his little feet and laugh. I bathed him in the bird bath in the summers!

LARMON. Did you? I never knew that!

CLARISSE. Yes! He loved it! When it was warm and it was hot I would do that! And there were beautiful birds, one of them had a flaming red head and polka dotted wings in black and white. He was very powerful, a bossy, powerful bird.

LARMON. How very nice, Clarisse!

CLARISSE. He was a boy the birds would allow to touch them. He held each bird in the palms of his hands and he kissed them.

LARMON. You're just being romantic.

CLARISSE. He put feathers under my pillow. All different kinds.

LARMON. Clarisse…

CLARISSE. It's true, Larmon.

LARMON. Who knows what's true?

CLARISSE. Don't be silly.

LARMON. Let us say only true things about the dead, Clarisse, only true things.

CLARISSE. The expression is actually: let us say only good things about the dead. *Nil nisi bonum de mortuis.* Nothing but good things about the dead.

LARMON. They meant kind things, not false things. There is always something kind to say. That doesn't make them false.

CLARISSE. When you can only say kind things, and no unkind things, you leave a lot out, and that is false.

LARMON. What unkind things are there to say about the boy?

CLARISSE. He's dead.

(Silence)

LARMON. I'll pay you for every true thing. I'll make you rich at our little funeral; every true thing you say about the boy I'll pay you.

CLARISSE. Is truth such a luxury, then?

LARMON. Yes, Clarisse dear, let's pretend it's very expensive. I'll pay you for every true thing you say at our little funeral.

CLARISSE. How much? How much will you pay me?

LARMON. One hundred. I'll pay you one hundred for every true thing you say.

CLARISSE. But how will you know if it's true?

LARMON. I will know.

CLARISSE. But what if you think it isn't true and it is?

LARMON. Then we'll call the man in the photograph.

CLARISSE. Does it have to be big or can it be small?

LARMON. It doesn't matter.

CLARISSE. Alright.

LARMON. Please begin.

CLARISSE. Alright. He died overseas.

LARMON. One hundred.

CLARISSE. He died in war.

LARMON. Two hundred.

CLARISSE. He...he...he wrote us letters sometimes.

LARMON. Three hundred.

CLARISSE. The letters were factual and lacking tenderness and he said he could hear screaming all the time and he said one time he thought guys were horsing around but they were being beheaded.

LARMON. Four hundred.

CLARISSE. He farted very loudly and thought it was funny.

LARMON. Five hundred.

CLARISSE. He...was in pieces. Not many people are in pieces.

LARMON. Seven hundred. For two true things.

CLARISSE. When he was little he couldn't be trusted around flowers. He ate them.

LARMON. Eight hundred.

CLARISSE. He was dead before he died, something already killed him.

LARMON. What does that mean?

CLARISSE. Will you pay me or not?

LARMON. Explain what that means.

CLARISSE. He hated his father.

LARMON. I won't pay for that!

CLARISSE. He was already dead!

LARMON. Let's stop this now, Clarisse.

CLARISSE. You've paid for it, Larmon. You've paid for it.

LARMON. Let's call that terrible man in the photograph. Look on the back and get the number. Tell him we're angry. Tell him we're very angry and we want our son back.

CLARISSE. Larmon, I'm sorry…

LARMON. *(Furious.)* Tell him, Clarisse. I'll tell him. Get the photograph and let's call him. The phone number is on that paper. Tell him he took our son and we want him back. Tell him they seduced our boy. Like in the Odyssey. Tell him our son is on the water and sirens are singing and we insist that they return him. I'll tell them. Get the number, Clarisse. Those damned damned liars! Those stupid men who believe in Other Stupid Men!

CLARISSE. Think, Larmon, think! Why would he even go? Why would he even want to go away? It's not that man's fault or his picture, Larmon. It's not that man's fault. He's too stupid for anything to be his fault. Why did the boy go away? Who would go where there is nothing but dying all day and praying you won't all night? We didn't give him anything, he didn't think he was anything, he thought he could become hairy feet and manly legs when he was away, he hated you, Larmon, he was able to hate those foreigners because he hated you.

LARMON. You just need to blame his death on someone you know!

CLARISSE. I need nothing!

LARMON. He did not hate me! They told him it was…

CLARISSE. Did you ever notice his legs before? How hairy and manly they were? Did you ever notice his legs before, Larmon?

LARMON. I…there were…I had many fishing trips with him…

CLARISSE. Now here is his leg.

LARMON. It's probably not his! They're liars!

CLARISSE. Now here is his leg. Let us admire his hairy manly leg and his metaphysical arch.

LARMON. Meta*tarsal.*

(Silence. They stare at the photograph once again.)

LARMON. Look at his ankle.

CLARISSE. There's no hair at all around a one-inch radius from the bone.

LARMON. I wonder why that is.

CLARISSE. The bone is so commanding, so majestic. The bone is the palace of a King, and the hairs are peasants, walking backwards away from the Great One's presence.

LARMON. You are so whimsical today.

CLARISSE. There's a shadow on the big toe.

LARMON. His big toe.

CLARISSE. It must be a bruise.

LARMON. A shame, really, the photo is not in color.

CLARISSE. I think it's better, dear.

LARMON. Why better?

CLARISSE. It just is. And another bruise on the shinbone.

LARMON. His shinbone. It must have been an explosion.

CLARISSE. You think so?

LARMON. Yes. A big explosion.

CLARISSE. I'm so sorry for him.

LARMON. Don't be sorry for him, don't be sorry for him.

CLARISSE. Let's bury him.

LARMON. Bury him…

CLARISSE. Let's bury him back where he came from.

LARMON. Clarisse…

CLARISSE. *(Taking photograph and crumpling it and tearing it.)* Let's bury him back where he came from.

LARMON. *(Grabbing for the photograph.)* Stop it! Give me that!

CLARISSE. Please, Larmon, please…

(CLARISSE gets up from the table after crushing and tearing photograph into a small ball of ruined pieces. She stands stiffly and quietly, then reaches into her clothing, under her skirt, inside her underpants, and begins stuffing the pieces into her crotch. When all the pieces are inside her skirt and panties, inside her body, she stops, exhausted. LARMON rises slowly, comes over to her, kneels down and puts his face where the photograph is. LIGHTS FADE DOWN VERY SLOWLY. End of play)

Act III

THE RICH SILK OF IT

(As lights come up, SHE is standing in a doorway, facing HE, who is standing upstage of her and to her right, so that she cannot really see him, but only feel him. He is holding a gun, pointed at her head, which can be merely his hand in the shape of a gun, the way children use their hands to play cops and robbers)

SHE. I'm so sorry, and you're trembling, you poor man, you beautiful man, I bet you've never killed anyone before. You planned this! You never plan anything! You poor boy! How responsible you must feel, like a little boy at his Confirmation, with all those people staring at him kneeling by the altar! You look like you're 10 years old. I haven't seen that shirt before. Did I give you that shirt? I can imagine the conversations you've had with yourself: I'm going to do this! I'm going to do this! You have that darkness in you, don't you, I've had my feet stuck in it like mud, so many nights. Darkness dresses up fancy in some people, the way it does in you; the way it borrows the clothes of extravagance, the ways of chattiness; kindness, big gestures. The way you buy drinks for everyone in a musty bar. Strangers. You know. The diamond you gave me.

27

I feel my Mother. My mother is upstairs. She's hearing this. I'm listening to my Mother listening! She's going to come down here and see me after you have shot me. Who is a mother who has seen the body of her dead child? Who is such a woman?

I love the way we sit outside in the yard in Brooklyn. Did you ever notice the mosquitoes? We have the most incredible mosquitoes in our yard, did you ever notice them? When we sit outside, and never get bitten! They're the size of small birds, very polite and silent. Never whining. I'd look at you and while you're talking I'd count the mosquitoes perched on strands of your hair, you have a whole corona of mosquitoes in your hair, big and feathery. They never bite us. I never got a single bite in that yard, except when we left it to get beer. Outside of that yard, they bite. We have in that yard in Brooklyn mosquitoes that live on something other than blood. What might that be? Can you think of what that might have been?

That diamond, I'm giving you back that diamond. Are you angry? You are. It's too beautiful, it just takes up too much of my time, forgive me. Rather than watch out for dangerous people or read a good book I stare at that diamond. The way it's cut. A hall of mirrors, it is. I just spend too much time. Tilting it back and forth, your mouth is trembling, I'm sorry: the way it parried light, the hardness of the stone shooting the light back heavenwards. It takes up all my time, that diamond. It makes me think of amusement parks, distorted mirrors, carnivals, cheap cameras, flashy neon lights. It thrills me in a very sad way. It's hot, that diamond, it's so hot.

You're taking me to the ballet, remember the ballet? We go to that ballet, and you're wearing those boots, the ones you got in Dallas, with the gun in one of them, and I'm thinking about the dancers' shoes, and yours, how they both come to such hard ends, at the toe, where the toes are, how hard they both are. And that swan, she keeps turning and turning, and that little red dot appears between her legs, and she's doing those turns, those fouettè turns, where the leg extends in front and then whips the body around, again and again, and with every turn the red spot gets larger and larger, the frantic turns, and that redness blooming like a flower, until it takes up the whole space under her torso, like a horizon, and then she raises her leg behind her, all the way up, so high, so slowly, it takes forever for her to raise that leg, as long as it takes for the sun to set or for the N train to come after midnight, and then she falls into the arms of that man she's dancing with, he's so passionate, that man, and he catches her! You seem so upset in that ballet, and I'm so deeply grateful to you for bringWing me there, and I love how she dances, so publicly fertile, that white swan! I'm such a sucker for the ballet! And now we've gone out and we laugh and laugh! Why are we laughing?

(Sounds of laughter, glasses clinking, voices; restaurant noise. ACTRESS is now a WAITRESS. MAN HOLDING GUN is now a BARTENDER; the gun is nowhere to be seen.)

WAITRESS. He told me that he failed his English class in high school because they had to write an essay explaining the line:

Man is born free yet he is everywhere in chains
And he wrote:

This is just too obvious to riff on
and gave the paper to the teacher. So the teacher says:
Are you sure you're finished?
and he says
Fuck, yes!
and walks out.

BARTENDER. He got that right, dude; he was right about that anyway.

WAITRESS. Yeah, but you got to give a little, you know.

BARTENDER. I wish you'd give a little.

WAITRESS. Baby, I've given my all.

BARTENDER. Not to me you haven't.

WAITRESS. Yes, baby I have.

BARTENDER. *(Laughing)* Yeah, where is it?

WAITRESS. Look under your apron, fish it out, baby, and pass it along! There's a lot of hungry girls in the world!

*(They laugh, and then morph. SCENE switches to ACTRESS
and BOYFRIEND on bed; lights darken)*

HE. Fucking asshole.

SHE. Stop thinking about it, darling, come here, let me hold you.

HE. Asshole. I'm a fucking asshole.

SHE. You didn't do anything.

HE. Damn fucking right. Didn't do anything. Went around it, fucking asshole.

SHE. Stop…

HE. I shoulda ended that shit, a man woulda ended that shit.

SHE. You didn't have time to think.

HE. Shit, I had so much fucking time, never passed so slowly as it did coming around, seeing this fucking animal, I saw that animal, that thing, I saw it and saw it and saw it like forever, man…

SHE. Remember, in Matthew: The light of the body is the eye…

HE. Matthew can fuck me, this body, fucking shit, it was lying there, writhing, it was just writhing there, couldn't move, its eyes, you didn't see this, you shoulda seen this, its eyes all glassed over and screaming at me, these eyes, it was in such pain, so much fucking pain, I shoulda ended it, I swerved around it, like this big S, around to the left and then back to the right again, avoided it, couldn't, I couldn't, I couldn't do it, then I hear this honking, right, guy behind me looking at me, starts honking, giving me the finger, because I fucking stopped, man, I didn't even know I stopped, I was stopped after this animal, right in front of it, just shaking, I thought I was driving but I was just sitting there shaking, I look in my mirror and the fucking thing's looking at me, I'm a fucking asshole, I couldn't do it, blood coming out of its eyes, and the guy behind me, he's laughing, then he's mad, he's honking, he starts honking, he's screaming get the fuck on, and it's that access road, right, that road leading off 54 onto the East/West, the fucking rigs, the trees turning color, the tops of trees, and the sun going down so the air's all linty and filled with like those little purple spots, right, and this thing, what the fuck was it, man, it was big, man, looked like a groundhog or some fucking thing, huge, man, like a small bear, or some shit, if I woulda got out and strangled it with my own hands, I shoulda used my hands, warm at least instead of the tread of a fucking Goodyear, and it couldn't move, writhing like that, it couldn't get up, fucking asshole, man…

SHE. What about that man?

HE. …and I think it made a sound, I think it made this horrible noise, like a moan, man, I keep hearing it, I think it made a sound, it made this sound…

SHE. That man, the man behind you, didn't he hit it? I'm sure he must have hit it.

HE. I don't know. No. I don't know. He rode over it with his wheels on either side of it, I couldn't really see, in that asshole Jeep…

SHE. You were compassionate, you didn't want to kill it, that is the only truth of this, please, baby.

HE. The truth ain't shit.

SHE. How can you say that?

HE. It ain't shit.

SHE. Honey…

HE. A man woulda ended it, even half a man.

(Lights down on HE, up on SHE.)

SHE. He offered me ten million dollars for my hands. He wanted to cut my hands off my arms and pay me for them. He said this. Just a month after I moved away, but it wasn't away, just Manhattan. He said silence wasn't a condition for this transaction, this sale, he called it a sale; he said I could call the police immediately and if he couldn't get away, couldn't flee with the hands from some airport, or some harbor, he'd pay for the hands that way too, in prison, all his life, with his life as well as his money, he'd pay for my hands. I told him: baby, what use would my hands be to you? He said, you touch me, you touch me. And he said: I can always be touched by you, I don't like to touch myself It made me think about the way that hands really serve only the one born with them; for who else do they bring the spoon come to the lips, or any tender thing? I told him no, and I laughed, but he said he'd come back for my hands.

(Lights crossfade down on SHE, up on HE, who stands crouched in some hideous distorted solitude.)

HE. I bought her this nightgown, fucking silk nightgown, black, with pink trim. Her body is like madness, it's like, new every day, never the same twice, it's like a new body every day, every time, it's madness. I bought her this nightgown, it was hot, I thought she'd really dig it, so she took it out of the box, man, and she smiled and said Thank You but I don't think it turned her on that much, anyway. She put it on then, and I practically tore it offa her, it wasn't on her back two seconds, and every night in August I made her put it on, and I thought, why am I being such an asshole, forcing her to wear the same shit every time we get it on, but it was just a way of recognizing her, it was so scary, fucking a different woman every night, that's what it felt like, so when she put that on, I remembered it was her, and her voice too, in the dark, when I couldn't see her, I could tell it was her, but looking at her, man, she fucking morphed and changed into weird people and shit. She was pretty, yeah, but always in a different way, I never knew which beauty I was seeing, or getting, or whatever, or who might come along and steal it, like not knowing which bank your money's in, or how much there is, or who has their hand in it. One night she fell asleep in it, in that fucking nightgown, and I dreamed she was drowning in the Ocean, and that Ocean was sex with this guy, or this creature, like some force almost, I don't know what it was, and I tried reaching out to her, like part of me knew it was a dream, but that kind of knowing didn't help me, I was scared shit, and I tried to reach for her but that silk was so slippery, it pushed my hand away, and I couldn't hold on, I felt so scared and like she didn't love me at all, and like I had misunderstood all the time what she was made of. When I was a little kid I thought you could sleep on a cloud if you could just get up there high enough, I guess all little kids think that, that you could lay down on it and sleep, and then the teacher told me that you couldn't do that, you'd fall right through it, that it was just broken-up little pieces of water and air, just vapors, and it couldn't hold you, and I was so lost on that, I lost everything on that, and that's how it felt trying to take hold of her in that nightgown, I couldn't get hold of her, and I never let her sleep in that shit again, I forbade her! First I can't hold her in the light, and then in the dark, even in the goddamn dark, I can't hold her.

(HE and SHE become WAITRESS and BARTENDER)

BARTENDER. He only wants you for your body.
WAITRESS. No, he wants me for his body.

HE. I love you.
SHE. I love you.
HE. I'm gonna marry you and be with you forever.
SHE. Forever isn't very long.
HE. It is long, it's forever.
SHE. Yes, but it goes by very quickly!

(SHE laughs, HE stares at her long and hard.)

SHE. Can I read your palm now?

HE. Not now.

SHE. *(Laughing)* C'mon!

HE. You can read other parts of me!

SHE. Give me your hand, Cassie taught me how to read your hand.

HE. Cassie's crazy.

SHE. No she's not, give me your hand.

HE. I wish I could cut you into tiny little pieces so I could master them one by one. Your lips, the inside of your wrists, your belly button, your calf muscles, your ankles, they look like upside-down parasols, the backs of your knees, the balls of your feet…all in separate pieces.

SHE. I'm only useful when I'm *attached* to myself.

HE. You're attached to me now!

SHE. Yes, I am, I am very attached to you! Give me your hand.

(HE and SHE become WAITRESS and BARTENDER)

BARTENDER. I'm really worried about him, that look in his eye, why is he coming here? He's here like every night, doesn't he have a job or something? Like when he walks in here his face seems to be sliding off his cheekbones, like it was painted on and it's peeling off in the rain, his eyes look like rocket holes. He seems insane, Ly, I don't like it. Do you want me to walk you home?

(CHURCH scene. HE is now PASTOR.)

SHE. I don't know how to bring him to prayer, and if he

doesn't come to prayer, I can't be with him.

PASTOR. Don't judge him harshly.

SHE. Oh Father, I don't judge him at all, but he seems so frightened and that scares me.

PASTOR. How has he scared you?

SHE. He said the other day he wants to cut me up into little pieces so he could understand me better, or something like that.

PASTOR. You are too much for most men, my dear one.

SHE. In what way?

PASTOR. Your beauty.

SHE. Am I so beautiful?

PASTOR. Are you?

SHE. He thinks I am.

PASTOR. It's written, in Matthew: Wherefore if thy hand or thy foot offend thee, cut them off, and cast them from thee: it is better for thee to enter into life halt or maimed, rather than having two hands or two feet to be cast into everlasting fire.

SHE. Do you think that's what will happen to me? That I'll be cast into everlasting fire?

PASTOR. Not to you, my beloved one. Not to you.

SHE. I'm just starting to understand this life. I feel like I'm just beginning to get it.

PASTOR. That's the first step on the journey towards full humility, towards the accepting of ignorance, and the placing of faith in God.

SHE. Can't I place my faith in God, *and* understand this life?

PASTOR. Those two are one and the same thing, my dear. You mention them in the same breath, and as your faith in God matures, you will not need to mention them at all.

SHE. But…

PASTOR. Bring him to church. Let me speak with him.

(Lights crossfade back to bedroom of HE and SHE.)

SHE. That's right. Stretch your hand out, palm up, and let me look…no! Not so tight like that, just gently, hold your hand open, so I can see all the lines! It's like a roadmap on Mapquest! So many lines, and there's a star for the destination, and a circle for the place you're starting from, but no way to connect the two! I can never read those maps on Mapquest; ooh, there! There's your Heart Line! Let me look at this. Hold still. See! This is the heart line, up here at the top! And yours doesn't stop, it goes right around your hand to the other side!

HE. I'm all heart, that means.

SHE. No, I think it means that you worship people! And then get disappointed because they're just mere mortals!

HE. None of my friends are mere mortals, we're all gods, and he-men, you know that!

SHE. And here is your Line of Children! Ooh, sweetheart, you're going to have three children! Or maybe just two! See, this vertical line is smaller than the other two, maybe this one will be conceived but not born, or maybe you'll just not be sure if you want to have a third one or not, it can symbolize uncertainty. And here's that fork! She talked about that fork at the end of this middle line, but I forgot what that means! I think it matters *where* it forks.

HE. Gotta be careful where you fork in this world!

SHE.…it matters, because…okay, right! This means you are a creative person, an inventor, an intuitor, that you see things intuitively, and deeply, and this is your Life Line, your line of life is very, very long, you'll live to be so old, my darling! You'll be really really old, and walk with a cane, and shake it at the children on the street to scare them off! You'll be so old and so beautiful! Your hands will shake and you'll have long white hair and listen to the Beatles! And pee a lot! And play bingo! And...

HE. *(His tone changes.)* I want to eat you whole without cutting you.

SHE. I wouldn't fit.

HE. You would fit.

SHE. I wouldn't...

HE. You haven't really seen inside me. There's so much room, baby, c'mere, touch me, take off your shirt, touch me down here, make a God outta me, c'mere, baby, touch me...

(Both roles of PASTOR and HE played by HE; conversation is quick and desperate and barely above a whisper.)

HE. Buy you a drink?

PASTOR. Right here, son, I have some wine.

HE. Buy you a drink?

PASTOR. Easy, son, easy, you're shaking.

HE. Dusty's, right down the street, it's my pleasure.

PASTOR. Are things alright?

HE. What? What did you say?

PASTOR. Are things alright at home?

HE. Great, things are great, can I buy you dinner, you been blowing out candles all day, come on, lemme buy you something.

PASTOR. No, no, son, thank you, my wife...

HE. You married? D'ja say you're married?

PASTOR. 29 years.

HE. What's that like, she still love you?

PASTOR. So she says, she says…

HE. You believe her? Believe it?

PASTOR. I always said…

HE. You believe it?

PASTOR. Yes, most days I do.

HE. And is the human spirit really immortal, is the soul really immortal?

PASTOR. Sometimes it is!

HE. What?

PASTOR. I mean…

HE. Knock knock!

PASTOR. What?

HE. Knock knock you're supposed to say Who's There.

PASTOR. Who's there?

HE. Rude interrupting cow.

PASTOR. Rude interrupt…

HE. *(Very loudly.)* MOOOOOOO!

PASTOR. Case in point; I see.

HE. Knock knock.

PASTOR. Who's there?

HE. Rude interrupting starfish.

PASTOR. But starfish don't make any…

HE. Fuck that, you hear me, fuck that.

PASTOR. Rude interrupting star…

*(HE takes his hand and, with fingers wide apart, places it all the
way over his own face, which is the face of the PASTOR.)*

PASTOR. Take your hand off my face, son

(This scene is identical to the opening scene, only now HE stands facing her, the gun pointed at her, and she can see him)

SHE. I think about hands alot, do you think about hands? Hands make me sad and they lift me up too, I'm a big follower of their mysteries; the hand that a little child puts on the person who carries her, the little hand, is it folded, or open? It sits on the person's shoulder, that little hand on the shoulder, or the chest, its stillness belying the movement of the eyes, the seeing, the listening to sounds: the hand on the body of the carrier. I remember my sister's children's hands on the breast they just fed from, the tender little supplicant hands! The hands of the woman who makes sandwiches at Subway, she probably just held a child, smoothed it's back, burped it, laid it down and now she deftly slices the flesh of a cow for my sandwich. I wonder if they consider the trembling fingers that open contraceptive devices, every time I see one of those spermicide tubes in its glossy paper cover I think: trembling hands, the trembling fingers that open this, in that moment; do they make them for those kinds of hands, fingers; do they realize, have they thought?

When I look at someone's hands, I feel like a spy, I see where the hands have been, I think: they've put in a tampon, they've shaped a sculpture, they've played piano in a bar, they've fingered somebody, they've counted bills quickly, with spit on the fingertips, they've cupped a match in the winter, or spooned each other in prayer.

And now look at your hand, holding that gun like that, is that the one you put in your boots or your pants all the time, where did you keep that gun? You always said you had one, but since I never saw it I thought it was a state of mind. Now I see. But look at your hand. Look at it now, it looks so graceful, and so upright, and if I pretend the gun isn't in that hand, if I erase that gun with my eye, it looks like sign language, like you're signing for the deaf a word that means Sex, or, no: it looks a sea anemone, or something with water moving around it. Or it looks like you're reaching to shake a hand, to shake someone's hand who you'd like to get to know. Who you feel is important. You like important people, I love your hands. Do you think about hands? Do you?

ACT IV

TIME IS THE MERCY OF ETERNITY

(A WOMAN lies in a plumped-up, elegantly-made, huge bed. It has matching pillow throws and comforter, and looks magnificent, almost edible. Next to the bed, facing her and in profile to the audience, is a stern-looking woman in a blazer and skirt. She stares at the WOMAN in the bed.)

WOMAN IN BED. If only it got more sunlight, I'm sure the whole thing would be more workable. You know, I walk by the neighbors and just stick my face in those flowers. Like those men who steal your shoes from your closet and smell them in private. They could steal your diamonds or your heart but what they want is your shoes. Those big bunches of flowers are like pantyhose or body parts. I just love to stick my face in them. I'm sure you've been through something like this yourself! I feel like such an outsider, but in a way it's delicious! Like a thief, a renegade! I just forage through the world and stick my face in the flowers of others! And don't think I haven't tried everything, I have! I even went to the local nursery, a woman from our town studied gardening with the Queen of England or some such dignitary! And she told me to try planting little shoots around the bush! Little boytoys or trophy wives for her to consort with! So I bought some of those and planted them right nearby, and still nothing! I went outside and I begged this bush for the favor of flowers, very polite-like! Then people say: it takes time, years even!

WOMAN IN BLAZER. Ma'am...

WOMAN IN BED. *(Continuing)* I met a man who told me: You're too nice! You don't beg for flowers, you don't pray for them, you threaten! You go out there with an axe! He said he and his wife had a flowering tree that wouldn't flower, and they went out there with an axe and stood in front of the tree like American Gothic with the pitchfork! And they staged a whole little play out there for her! The tree was the audience! Can you believe that? And they did an entire presentation, the man said: What shall we do with this tree? It will not flower! And the woman waved the axe, saying: I chop her down! I take her down right now! They were Slavic, that's why they talked like that, with the verbs in the present tense! And she even gave the axe a good sway and heave! And they stood there talking like that, and two days later, BINGO! Flowers this way and that!

WOMAN IN BLAZER. Look...

WOMAN IN BED. Is that your cell phone ringing?

WOMAN IN BLAZER. Ma'am, I'm going to have to...

WOMAN IN BED. Is it? Is that your cell phone? I hear something ringing!

WOMAN IN BLAZER. Ma'am, I cannot allow this to continue. I have already called the...

WOMAN IN BED. Who? Who did you call? You called someone?

WOMAN IN BLAZER. Ma'am, I have called security. You cannot lie in this bed, it is a store display and is not for customer use. I have asked you repeatedly...

WOMAN IN BED. Aha! You feel if you threaten me, I'll

flower! You're swinging the axe!

WOMAN IN BLAZER. Security is on the way down here, ma'am, and you will have to answer to…

WOMAN IN BED. Oh, I've distressed you! I'm so sorry. Listen, I should have told you. Forgive me! I should have told you…at least we're not on a cell phone! That's a relief! Haha! I should have told you! I've bought this place! I've bought the whole store! With my credit card! I put the whole store on my credit card! It was a MasterCard! I own this place! I am the Master Card of this place! I'm now the owner of this place! This bed, that urn, this weird-looking device over there, those purple dinner napkins! That divan with the cushions! All of it! So we have all the time in the world to have this conversation! I bought this store just so I could lie in this bed and tell you these things. I like you. I like how you look and how hard you try! You look so remorseless in your suit and even your face is wearing a suit, your eyes are the blazer and your chin is the skirt! You're well-suited! I am not well-suited, you see, and that's why I wanted to talk to you! I bought this whole store just so I could talk to you! Will you sit down? No, you are not a person who will sit down, I'll have to talk quickly! Tell me, do you like your cell phone?

WOMAN IN BLAZER. Excuse me?

WOMAN IN BED. Do you like your cell phone? Does it give you good service? How many minutes do you get?

WOMAN IN BLAZER. You don't seem to understand me, ma'am, you are to get up and leave this bed right now! I cannot stand here!

WOMAN IN BED. Doesn't it confuse you sometimes, when you've been talking for a long time to someone on your cell phone, telling them something important or secret or desperate, and you realize suddenly that the person to whom you are speaking is not there? It's painful not to know when you lost someone! Losing someone is always hard, but not to know when!

WOMAN IN BLAZER. I…I…I…I always know when…

WOMAN IN BED. And even if you do know when! Such nonsense! I lost my son to a man who hated him, my daughter to a man who loved her, and my husband to the stuffiness and congestion in his own heart! It just blew up or something! Such nonsense!

WOMAN IN BLAZER. …because my phone makes a sound. A certain sound. I always know when.

WOMAN IN BED. That must be very comforting. Very helpful.

WOMAN IN BLAZER. I…yes…sometimes…I...dread…I…

WOMAN IN BED. What's inside your purse? What do you carry in your purse? Show me!

(WOMAN IN BLAZER stares at her, then walks away abruptly and in profound confusion, exiting stage right; WOMAN IN BED continues speaking to her throughout her absence, turning in the direction of her EXIT, and is delighted but not surprised when she returns, becoming simultaneously calmer and more richly emotional.)

WOMAN IN BED. Oh, you're just worried that I'm taking up too much of your time and you'll be fired, please don't worry! I am your employer now! Don't be in such a hurry, dear! In fact… *(Nearly in a whisper.)* Did you ever hear of this idea:

Time is the mercy of eternity.

(WOMAN IN BLAZER re-enters timidly but in some strange hunger)

I've been thinking about that for 40 years.
Time is the mercy of eternity.

(A pause.)

WOMAN IN BLAZER. *(Shaking)* Eternity is a perfume. As is Obsession, Ambush, Joy, and Insolence.
WOMAN IN BED. Is there Mercy?
WOMAN IN BLAZER. No.

(Pause)

WOMAN IN BED. *(Continuing)* I was young when I read that somewhere, very young, and it was part of this very long thing, they made us read it, it went on and on, you see, I don't like things that go on and on. But in that mess, that big junkpile of words and letters and periods and capitals and strophes I found that ravishing thing:
Time is the mercy of eternity,
And it's that that I wanted to talk to you about. You are such a lovely woman!

WOMAN IN BLAZER. You don't even know me! You...
WOMAN IN BED. You see, I do know you, because I want to! Desire is a form of invention! Now, what do you think that means? Time is the mercy of eternity
WOMAN IN BLAZER. I can see the security guard. He has a gun and he's coming.

WOMAN IN BED. Is that what you think it means? That there's a man coming to end this moment with a gun?

WOMAN IN BLAZER. I have no idea…ma'am, you can't…

WOMAN IN BED. Everybody in the class said it meant that eternity was a big relief because it meant you finally had enough time for everything. But I don't think so, I never thought so, I thought it meant…something else. What do you think?

WOMAN IN BLAZER. No one ever..

WOMAN IN BED. I thought it meant…let's see! I thought…I thought it meant…that time was divided up into very little pieces, because that's the only way it can seem to be owned or mastered, to belong to me, or to you! Eternity is claustrophobic, you see, because it's too open, too big, there are no soda machines or cigarettes in sight! Nothing but open space for thousands of miles, like in Death Valley! Where there's nothing for miles, but as you drive, for hundreds of miles in the night, you see, on the horizon, blinking with such sadness:

COTTONTAIL RANCH

…and that sign just blinks and blinks and miles and miles of nothing but thirst and the thought of the cottontail ranch. I actually went there. I went there because I couldn't stand eternity! I'm sure you understand what I'm talking about! And I rang the bell after hours and miles and hours and miles and a woman with lipstick that extended below and above her lips saw me and said:

honey this is a bordello and women are not allowed!

and she slammed the door. But were I a man, I could have bought an hour, bought an hour with that sad Latina lady, I saw her lying there, don't you see, on a big bed, I saw her there, all plumped up, just as you're seeing me now! Time is the mercy of eternity. I'm telling you, that's why I bought this place! To tell you that. To discuss that idea with you in deepest leisure! To hear your thoughts about that. You can buy minutes for your cell phone, or an hour at a hotel, did you know that some hotels will sell you an hour…a woman will sell you an hour…a night… time is the mercy of eternity, don't you see…it's human-sized pieces of eternity! That's very gracious, I think! Clever, even! Like this bed! I can understand this bed! I can't understand Hell! But this bed I understand!

WOMAN IN BLAZER. *(Frantic)* He's coming through the second set of doors!

WOMAN IN BED. Come in this bed with me! We have all afternoon, we have nighttime, we have the hours between pieces of the earliest morning with no windows and no words and no people, come into this bed, let's sell the morning an hour with us!

(SECURITY GUARD enters and stands SR of women, hand on his gun. WOMAN IN BLAZER is almost visibly torn in half by the two people with whom she is sharing the stage. She nods to the GUARD, who takes a step closer to the women.)

WOMAN IN BLAZER. *(To WOMAN IN BED.)* You are making fun of me, you want me to be fired! You have not purchased this store, I..I..checked with the Central Office, and you are trespassing on this property. You are guilty of completely disorderly conduct and loitering and these are criminal offenses. If you do not get up AT ONCE, I will ask this guard to physically remove you from our premises. The police will arrest you and you will be taken away by force.

WOMAN IN BED. Things that happen by force can't be said to really happen.

WOMAN IN BLAZER. They are the only things that really happen! GET OUT OF HERE! IMMEDIATELY!

WOMAN IN BED. *(Suddenly and immutably decisive.)* Oh, oh…I'm flowering! My darling! You're swinging the axe, and I'm blooming! *(Grabs WOMAN IN BLAZER, pulls her close and kisses her deeply on the mouth. Murmuring:)* Can you tell…can you tell…I'm blooming…thank you…I'm blooming…

(The embrace between the women deepens in intensity. WOMAN IN BLAZER has fallen into the embrace as if it were a body of water; she is given to it and taken by it in a way that seems both gently humorous and completely inevitable. SECURITY GUARD sits down, as if to wait for a storm to pass, staring off into the distance, hand idly on his gun, while the women kiss)

LIGHTS FADE

END OF PLAY